I'm Afraid Your Teddy Is in the Principal's Office

To Roseann Manley, my fourth-grade teacher,
and to teachers everywhere
J. D.

To the Sunshine Sisters, Lenora & Hazel
S. N.

Text copyright © 2020 by Jancee Dunn
Illustrations copyright © 2020 by Scott Nash

First edition 2020

Library of Congress Catalog Card Number pending
ISBN 978-1-5362-0198-7

20 21 22 23 24 25 LGO 10 9 8 7 6 5 4 3 2 1

Printed in Vicenza, Italy

This book was typeset in Chowderhead.
The illustrations were created digitally.

Candlewick Press
99 Dover Street
Somerville, Massachusetts 02144

visit us at www.candlewick.com

I'm Afraid Your Teddy Is in the Principal's Office

Jancee Dunn

illustrated by Scott Nash

CANDLEWICK PRESS

Now, I know that you've always been a good student. In fact, I believe this is the first time you've ever been to my office.

But I'm afraid your teddy has been naughty today.

Somehow, earlier this morning, he contacted a
number of his stuffed animal pals and had them
sneak into children's backpacks all across town.

Once they were at school, they waited in the cubbies
until all the children went to an assembly.

That's when the party began.

Their first stop was the cafeteria. Mr. Krimple tells me the cafeteria manager was not happy about how the lunch shift went. For one thing, instead of dirty dishes, all they left behind was a life-size teddy molded out of sloppy joe filling.

And I'm told the animals made up a new game called Pizza Fling. Can you figure out how it was played? Yes, I thought so.

It seems they also made wigs out of the spaghetti. And mustaches. And beards.

How do we know they did this? Because they signed their names on the wall. Teddy used ketchup. The elephant chose mustard. It seems Sock Monkey prefers ranch dressing.

I must ask you not to laugh, Mr. Krimple.

After that, they spent some time in the gym.

Coach Sherman tried to get things under control.
He didn't have much luck.

I've been at this school for twenty years, and I
thought I'd seen everything. But this is a first.
This is a first!

Next the gang headed for the music room. I don't know where your teddy managed to find a bottle of bubbles, but he poured it into the instruments. Can you guess what happened during band practice?

After that, they were somehow able to get inside the teachers' lounge.

This has always been the school's most top-secret room. We wouldn't want the teachers to be, ah . . . *interrupted* as they're preparing their next lesson, would we?

It seems that the animals' last stop was the art department. I'm told that Teddy took every bottle of glue in the supply cabinet and made a trap for the art teacher, Mr. Waggenbottom.

Mr. Krimple, if you can't control yourself, I must ask you to please leave the room.

Then the animals rolled around in the finger paint.
Finger paint, need I remind you, is for fingers,
not bodies.

At that point, they must have known we were looking for them.

So they took a bag of pipe cleaners, twisted them together to form a rope, and escaped out the window.

And now I am sorry to say that they must face the consequences.
We'll see what your teddy has to say for himself.

You know, I used to have
a teddy bear once.

He looked a lot like you.

Oh, Teddy — don't look so sad. I'm sure you didn't mean to make so much mischief.

As we principals like to say, there are no naughty bears — only naughty behavior. Now, how about a hug?

Thank you, Teddy. Now you can all go home. I'm sure I won't be seeing you in my office again anytime soon!